This Is
Me

Poetry by Doug Sloss

This Is

Me ©

ISBN 9798620687176

Printed in the USA

Andre Renee Writes ®

www.arwrites.com

Dedication

I would like to dedicate this to the family and friends who have supported me and who continue to support me in this crazy journey called life. Thank you to everyone who has read or will read this. It was not easy to put myself out there like this. I really appreciate you.

Table of Contents

THE SEARCH

OH, HOW I LONG FOR THE TIME WHEN WE CAN BE TOGETHER

DAY AFTER DAY, I WAIT FOR YOUR EMBRACE

YOU HOLD MY HEART

I WANT TO LAY BESIDE YOU UNDER THE STARS ON A WARM
SUMMER NIGHT, A GENTLE BREEZE CARESSING OUR INTERLOCKED
HANDS

AND WHEN IT RAINS, I WANT TO DANCE WITH YOU IN IT UNTIL WE
ARE SOAKED

WHEN IT'S COLD, I WANT TO KEEP YOU WARM

I KNOW YOU ARE OUT THERE

YOU MAY BE NEAR, YOU COULD BE FAR

TO FIND YOU, NO DISTANCE IS TOO FAR

YOU ARE WHO I'VE BEEN PRAYING FOR

AND ONCE WE ARE UNITED, ONLY DEATH WILL CAUSE ME TO LET
GO

I ACCEPT YOUR MISTAKES AND FLAWS

ANY PROBLEMS WE HAVE IN LIFE, I KNOW WE CAN FACE THEM ALL
TOGETHER

WHEN I THINK OF US, I WANT IT TO BE PURE

SO WAIT FOR ME AND I WILL FIND YOU SOON

YOUR FUTURE HUSBAND

YOU ARE NOT ALONE

YOU ARE NOT ALONE

THOUGH AT TIMES YOU FEEL LIKE YOU MAY BE

JUST KNOW THAT IT WILL EVENTUALLY WORK OUT

YOU WILL SEE BETTER DAYS

AT TIMES YOU FEEL NEGLECTED

IT SEEMS LIKE NOBODY CARES

AND YOU FEEL SO DISRESPECTED

PEOPLE WHO YOU THOUGHT CARED WEREN'T THERE

CAST YOUR CARES ON JESUS

HE WILL SET YOU FREE

THERE'S NOTHING HE CAN'T DO

HE SEES AND KNOWS ALL

YOU ARE NOT ALONE

GOD IS RIGHT THERE WAITING

HE WILL CARRY YOU THROUGH THE STORM

YOU ARE NOT ALONE

AT TIMES YOU MAY NOT SEE

JUST TRUST THAT GOD IS WORKING

IT WILL TURN IN YOUR FAVOR

YOU ARE NOT ALONE

FOR EVERY TEAR THAT YOU'VE CRIED

HE ALREADY KNOWS WHY

HE SEES AND HE CARES

YOU ARE NOT ALONE

WORDS

THE POWER OF WORDS

PLEASE DON'T TAKE THEM LIGHTLY

THEY CAN UNITE OR DIVIDE

TAKE AWAY SELF-ESTEEM

INSTILL GREAT PRIDE

WHY IS THIS?

THE POWER OF WORDS

GOD USED THEM TO SPEAK EVERYTHING INTO EXISTENCE

HOW POWERFUL WORDS ARE

THEY CAN HEAL OR HURT

CAUSE MISERY OR DELIGHT

PAIN OR PLEASURE

IF WORDS ARE LIKE BULLETS

THEN THE TONGUE MUST BE A GUN

IF WE AREN'T USING WORDS TO PROTECT

DESTRUCTION AND CHAOS IS WHAT'S NEXT

THAT IS THE POWER OF WORDS

WHEN I'M WITH YOU

WHEN I'M WITH YOU

THE SUN SEEMS TO SHINE A LITTLE BRIGHTER

THE AIR SEEMS TO GET A LITTLE LIGHTER

THE BIRDS SEEM TO FLY A LITTLE HIGHER

WHEN I'M WITH YOU

WHEN I'M WITH YOU

MUSIC SEEMS TO SOUND A LITTLE SMOOTHER

SWEETS SEEM TO TASTE A LITTLE SWEETER

THE GRASS FEELS A LITTLE SOFTER

WHEN I'M WITH YOU

HOLDING YOUR HAND

OR CAUGHT IN A HUG'S EMBRACE

YOU MEAN SO MUCH TO ME

NO ONE CAN TAKE YOUR PLACE

TIME SEEMS TO FLOW A LITTLE FASTER

HAPPY TIMES PRODUCE MORE LAUGHTER

LIFE SEEMS TO HAVE FEWER ACTORS

WHEN I'M WITH YOU

THE STRUGGLE

DAILY I TRY

DAILY I FAIL

TRYING TO WIN OVER MY FLESH

LOCKED UP, NO BAIL

TRYNA STAY PRAYED UP

MY SIN HAS ME CHAINED UP

I KNOW WE NEED TO GO THROUGH A BREAKUP

MY LIFE REALLY NEEDS A CHANGE UP

NOW YOU MAY THINK IT'S STRANGE

BUT I REFUSE TO REMAIN CAGED UP

CONTINUE TO GET BANGED UP

DAILY I FALL, BUT I'M ALWAYS TRYNA STAY UP

THOUGH SIN MAY HAVE ME BOUND

I KNOW I WON'T ALWAYS BE AROUND

MY FREEDOM WILL COME TO ME

I WILL HAVE VICTORY

<u>REGRET</u>

IF ONLY IT WAS SOMEONE ELSE

SOMEONE WHO COULD BOTH ACCEPT AND RETURN

I THOUGHT I MADE THE RIGHT CHOICE

I THOUGHT YOU WERE THE ONE

WE MIGHT AS WELL BE STRANGERS

BET EVEN NOW I CAN'T STOP CARING

LOVE IS CRUEL

WHY PRETEND TO BE FRIENDS?

IF ONLY I COULD GO BACK AND UNDO US

I HOPE YOU FIND SOMEONE WHO YOU CAN LOVE AS
MUCH AS I LOVE YOU, RETURNED

AS OF NOW I AM DONE

NO MORE PRETENDING

WE ARE JUST STRANGERS

NOTHING MORE, NOTHING LESS

REVEAL

SHOW ME THE SIDE OF YOU THAT NO ONE ELSE GETS TO SEE

EVERY SIDE OF YOUR HEART

LET ME BE THE ONE WHO SEES

I WANT TO GET LOST IN YOUR EYES

GAZE INTO THEM LIKE I'M STARING AT THE MOON

WATCHING THEM LIKE THE SUNRISE

I WANT TO SEE IT ALL

THE GOOD AND THE BAD

YOU CAN SHOW ME EVERYTHING

THE HAPPY FACES AND THE SAD

I COULD NEVER ASK WITHOUT GIVING ANYTHING IN RETURN

SO IF YOU SHOW ME YOU

THEN I'LL SHOW YOU ME

IS THAT FAIR?

I'LL GIVE YOU MY HEART

MY MIND

MY LOVE

MY TIME

DON'T BE AFRAID

I KNOW IT'S NOT EASY

I REALIZE I'M ASKING A LOT

NOT TRYING TO BE CHEESY

IF MY HEART HAD A SONG

YOU WOULD BE THE MELODY

MY ACTIONS WOULD BE THE VOICE THAT SINGS IT

I KNOW I'M NOT PERFECT

AND I'M NOT EXPECTING YOU TO BE

BUT YOU CAN TRUST AND BELIEVE MY AFFECTION

I'LL ALWAYS BE HONEST WITH YOU

JUST BE TRUE WITH ME

IT'S NOT JUST ABOUT THE ROMANCE

THE SOFT MUSIC OR THE SLOW DANCE

I'LL TAKE THE RAINY DAYS

TREASURE THE STORMY NIGHTS

WE MAY FIGHT

MAY BICKER

PROBABLY ARGUE

BUT WE WILL WORK IT OUT

SO PLEASE LET ME SEE

TRUST ME, I CAN TAKE IT

I KNOW YOUR HEART MAY BE FRAGILE

BUT YOU HAVE TO TRUST THAT I WON'T BREAK IT

SHOW ME THE SIDE OF YOU THAT NO ONE ELSE SEES

ACCEPT IT

THE LONELINESS SEEMS OVERWHELMING

AT TIMES IT DRAGS ME DOWN

HARD TO OVERCOME IT

BUT I ACCEPT IT

SOMETIMES I WELCOME IT WITH OPEN ARMS

IT'S THE COMPANY I SEEK

THAT FRIEND THAT I'VE LONGED FOR

AND I ACCEPT IT

PEOPLE TRY TO CHASE IT AWAY

FOR THEM THAT MAY WORK

BUT LONELY FOLLOWS ME LIKE A SHADOW

AND I ACCEPT IT

LONELY, I DON'T MIND IT

SOMETIMES LONELY AND I ARE HAPPY

UNTIL I IMAGINE A HAPPY LIFE WITHOUT LONELY

AND I ACCEPT IT

BUT SOONER OR LATER

LONELY WILL BE LONELY WITHOUT ME

AND I ACCEPT IT

CLOSURE

IT FEELS AS THOUGH WE HAVE TRULY ENDED

WHAT WAS ONCE THERE SEEMS TO BE GONE, NEVER AGAIN TO RETURN

MAYBE IT NEVER EXISTED AT ALL

YET HERE I AM, WAITING AND SEARCHING

HOPING THAT ONE DAY WE CAN PICK UP WHERE WE LEFT OFF

I FEEL LIKE THERE'S SOMETHING MISSING BETWEEN US

LIKE TALKING WITH A STRANGER WHO DOESN'T QUITE TRUST ME

WHO KNOWS? MAYBE IT HURTS BECAUSE I STILL WANT THERE TO BE AN "US"

YET NO MATTER HOW MUCH I WANT IT, IT'S USELESS IF YOU DON'T FEEL THE SAME

I COULD NEVER FORCE YOU TO STAY WHEN YOU DON'T WANT TO

I DON'T WANT TO CARE AT TIMES

I FIND MYSELF REMINISCING ABOUT YOUR BEAUTIFUL SMILE AND HOLDING YOU IN MY ARMS

REGARDLESS OF WHAT HAPPENS, I WILL BOTH SUPPORT AND PRAY FOR YOUR STRENGTH AND WELL-BEING

EVEN IF IT'S NOT WITH ME, I DESIRE THAT YOU FIND HAPPINESS AND LIVE A WONDERFUL LIFE

CONDOLENCES

AS WE STRUGGLE TO ACCEPT THE EMPTINESS YOUR ABSENCE HAS

CAUSED

WE REMINISCE ON ALL THE MEMORIES WE HAVE SHARED

YOUR DEATH HAS LEFT A GAP IN ALL OF OUR HEARTS THAT

MEMORIES STRUGGLE TO FILL

YOUR PAIN HAS ENDED AND YOUR WORK IS DONE

EVEN IN DEATH YOU STILL MANAGE TO TOUCH OUR LIVES, FOREVER

CHANGING US

AND IF TIME HEALS ALL WOUNDS THEN MAY THE SCARS SERVE AS A

REMINDER OF WHO YOU WERE AND THE IMPACT YOU MADE

GOD WANTED YOU BACK AND WE ARE FOREVER GRATEFUL FOR THE

TIME HE ALLOWED US TO HAVE WITH YOU

MAY THE ANGELS GUIDE YOU TO YOUR ETERNAL REST AND KNOW

THAT YOU WILL BE GREATLY MISSED

DEPRESSION

THE SADNESS SEEMS ETERNAL

THE VOID IN MY HEART SEEMS TO EXPAND

I TRY TO FIND REASONS TO KEEP GOING

BUT IT JUST FEELS SO HARD TO STAND

PEOPLE TRY TO ASK WHAT'S WRONG

I SMILE AND SAY "NOTHING"

HOPING DEEP DOWN INSIDE THAT THEY CAN'T TELL I'M BLUFFING

I JUST WANT TO BE ALONE

SILENCE IS MY FRIEND, MY COMPANION

I LAY AWAKE AT NIGHT JUST THINKING

WHEN WILL THE PAIN END?

ELEMENTS OF LOVE

TO ME YOU ARE LIKE THE RAIN

CLEANSING AND ABLE TO BRING LIFE TO THE BARREN
HOLLOW OF MY HEART

TO ME YOU ARE LIKE THE WIND

BLOWING AWAY THE LONELINESS THAT HAS TAKEN ROOT
IN MY LIFE

TO ME YOU ARE LIKE THE EARTH

A SOLID FOUNDATION ON WHICH I CAN DEPEND,

FOREVER NURTURING AND BOUNTIFUL IN ALL THAT YOU
PRODUCE

TO ME YOU ARE LIKE FIRE

ABLE TO BRIGHTEN THE HIDDEN RECESSES IN THE
SHADOW OF MY HEART

TO ME YOU ARE LIKE LIGHTNING

POWERFUL, MAGNIFICENT, AND FULL OF BEAUTY

TO ME YOU ARE LIKE THE MOON

ILLUMINATING MY DARKEST OF NIGHTS

TO ME YOU ARE LIKE THE SUN

PROVIDING WARMTH AND NEW OPPORTUNITIES

TO ME YOU ARE THE SUM OF ALL THE ELEMENTS THAT
MAKE UP MY HEART

ENIGMA

I AM A TREE HIDING IN A FOREST

YOU WANT TO KNOW WHO I AM?

START EXPLORING

KNOWLEDGE IS POWER

THE MORE YOU KNOW

THE GREATER YOUR ADVANTAGE

I LEARNED LONG AGO THAT TRUST EASILY GIVEN

IS A HEART THAT'S EASILY HURT

AND WOUNDS HEAL SLOWLY

WHO I AM AND WHAT I CHOOSE TO SHOW

THE FACE YOU SEE

AND THE ONE YOU KNOW

MAYBE THEY ARE DIFFERENT

EXPERIENCE IS THE BEST TEACHER

LIFE IS A TEST

AM I FAKE?

NOT AT ALL

BUT ONLY A FOOL SHOWS THE WORLD THEIR ALL

I CHOOSE TO BE AN ENIGMA

FIRST MEETING

AS I LOOK INTO YOUR EYES

I STARE IN AWE, BEWILDERED AND AT A LOSS FOR WORDS

CAPTIVATED, I TRY TO SPEAK

BUT MY WORDS ARE QUICK TO FLEE

SECONDS FEEL LIKE HOURS

YET ALL I CAN DO IS STARE INTO YOUR EYES

"SAY THIS," "DO THAT," MY MIND ORDERS

YET STILL I STARE INTO YOUR EYES

EYES THAT ARE SOFT YET STRONG

SILENTLY MY HEART RACES BUT MY FACE REMAINS CALM

"HELLO," I MANAGE TO UTTER OUT

NOW I'M WORRIED I'VE MADE A BAD IMPRESSION

I FREEZE, STILL STARING INTO YOUR EYES

WORRYING AND WAITING FOR A RESPONSE

CAUGHT IN THIS MOMENT THAT FEELS LIKE AN ETERNITY

I WAIT....

FUTURE BOO

THE MORE I WAIT FOR YOU, THE HARDER IT GETS

I MAY NOT HAVE EVEN MET YOU

YET HERE I AM, MISSING YOU

WORDS DON'T DO MY FEELINGS JUSTICE

WHO I LOVE, I CANT SEE

SOMETIMES I GET ANGRY WHEN I REALIZE ALL THE TIME
I'VE POSSIBLY MISSED IN YOUR EYES

ALL THE TIME WE HAVE MISSED

WE HAVE TO MAKE UP FOR IT

THE LOVE I HAVE

TRUST ME, IT'S VERY WORTH IT

ALL THIS TIME WITHOUT YOU

I'M BORED WITH IT

I SWEAR I'M NOT LYING

IT'S THE ABSOLUTE TRUTH

AND EVERY DAY I'LL CLAIM YOUR SWEET LIPS

TO ME THEY ARE JUST DIVINE

I WANT TO WRITE OUR NAME IN THE STARS

KEEP YOU SAFELY IN MY ARMS

YOU AND I, JUST CALL IT DESTINY

BEING AROUND YOU, IT BRINGS OUT THE BEST IN ME

LOOKING FOR YOU GETS SO VERY HARD

BUT I KNOW YOU WILL BE WORTH IT

<u>HELP</u>

IT'S REALLY HARD SOMETIMES TO WIN

FACING DAILY CONFRONTATIONS WITH SIN

MY SIN IS MY PRISON

I WANT BAIL

I DON'T LOSE EVERY BATTLE

BUT WHEN I DO,

CONDEMNATION SETS IN

I HATE MY SIN

I TRY SO HARD TO SHAKE IT

BUT IT'S LIKE IT HAS MY SCENT

IS IT ONLY ME?

EVERYONE ELSE SEEMS LIKE THEY ARE PERFECT

YET HERE I AM, CAUGHT IN SINS' GRAVE

THEY'RE READY TO THROW THE DIRT IN

I KNOW WE ALL HAVE OUR STRUGGLES

BUT WHY AM I FOLLOWED BY SIN AND HIS BEST FRIEND TROUBLE?

DYING DAILY,

YEAH, I DID THAT

IT WORKED FOR A WHILE BUT TEMPTATION CAUSED ME TO FALL
BACK

I FEEL ALONE, NO HELPING HAND

I WONDER, IS THIS HOW DANIEL FELT IN THE LION'S DEN?

ON SUNDAYS EVERYTHING IS FINE

THEN MONDAY COMES WITH TEMPTATION

I START TO LOSE SIGHT

BUT I RESIST

BECAUSE GOD SHOULD BE WORTH MORE TO ME THAN SOME TEMPORARY SIN

BUT THE WEEK GOES ON

THE BATTLE GETS A LITTLE HARDER

MY LIGHT SEEMS TO FADE

GOD, I NEED MORE POWER

I NEED YOU TO MAKE A WAY

IF IT'S SINNING AGAINST YOUR NAME

THAT'S SOMETHING I WANT NO PART OF

BUT IT'S ONLY TUESDAY

THE BATTLE WITH MY FLESH SEEMS TO LAST A LITTLE LONGER

GOD, I WANT TO DO YOUR WILL, SEEK YOUR FACE, AND PRAISE YOU

EVERYTIME I SLIP, I FEEL TOO ASHAMED TO SAY YOUR NAME

BUT GOD I AM TRYING

DAILY READING, PRAYING, AND FASTING

WHY DO I STILL SLIP EVEN WHEN I'M PUTTING ALL THIS TIME IN?

AT TIMES I'M UNSURE IF MY PRAYERS ARE EVEN GETTING HEARD

SILENCE IS ALL I SEEM TO HEAR

SO I GO BACK AND READ YOUR WORD

THEN I FAINTLY HEAR "TRUST IN THE LORD AND DON'T EVER GIVE UP"

"IN THE END YOU WILL BE VICTORIOUS IF YOU'RE UNDER THE BLOOD"

"IT WILL BE HARD AT TIMES BUT WITH HIS DEATH WE HAVE OVERCOME"

HERE WITH YOU

BEING HERE WITH YOU

IT'S BEEN A DREAM COME TRUE

I'M SO IN LOVE WITH YOU

I WANT OUR LOVE TO LAST FOREVER

LIFE IS SHORT

I WANT TO SPEND IT WITH YOU

IF OUR LIVES ARE BUT A MOMENT

THEN WE SHALL MAKE A MOMENT LAST A LIFETIME

I LOVE YOU

YOU ARE MY DREAM COME TRUE

I AM SO CAUGHT UP IN YOU

ENAMORED, I'M WITH YOU 'TIL THE END

NOW I KNOW EVERY DAY WON'T BE SUNSHINE

BUT WE WON'T HAVE CONSTANT RAIN EITHER

I'LL BE THERE THROUGH THOSE DARK NIGHTS

AND WHEN WE EXPERIENCE THE HAPPINESS AND THE PAIN

AND IF OUR LIVES LAST BUT A MOMENT

WE WILL MAKE THAT MOMENT LAST A LIFETIME

YOU AND ME

ME AND YOU

TOGETHER THERE IS NOTHING WE CAN'T CONQUER

SO TAKE A LEAP OF FAITH

GRAB MY HAND

IN THIS LIFE WE WILL BE TOGETHER THROUGH THICK AND THIN

AND IF OUR LIVES LAST BUT A MOMENT

WE WILL MAKE THE MOMENT LAST A LIFETIME

HURTING

THESE WORDS I HAVE FEEL USELESS

THEY CAN'T EXPRESS HOW I FEEL

MY MIND TELLS ME TO FEEL LESS

GIVE MY HEART A CHANCE TO HEAL

DON'T WANT THE MEMORIES

FEELS LIKE I WASTED TIME

I'VE GIVEN UP ON LOVE

DON'T WANT IT ON MY MIND

EVERYTHING YOU SAID TO ME

TELL ME, WAS IT JUST A LIE?

FAKING FEELINGS

LEADING ME ON

I DON'T KNOW HOW TO HEAL FROM THIS

I WANT THE PAIN TO LEAVE

HOW CAN I TRY TO FAKE A SMILE?

ALL I FEEL IS GRIEF

I LOVE YOU MORE

MORE THAN THE MOON LOVES THE NIGHT SKY

MORE THAN THE SUN LOVES TO SHINE

I LOVE YOU MORE

MORE THAN A DOG LOVES HIS BONE

MORE THAN THE SONGBIRD LOVES THEIR SONG

I LOVE YOU MORE

MORE THAN GAMBLERS LOVE THEIR DICE

MORE THAN A PENGUIN LOVES THE ICE

I LOVE YOU MORE

AND WHEN THE HARD TIMES COME

WHEN IT SEEMS LIKE WE'RE DONE

NO MATTER THE FIGHTS WE WILL HAVE

ALWAYS REMEMBER THAT I LOVE YOU MORE

I REALLY LOVE YOU

I NEVER WANT TO GO ANOTHER DAY WITHOUT YOU

I REALLY NEED YOU,

YOU ARE SO IMPORTANT AND NOBODY ELSE WILL DO

SO JUST TAKE MY HAND

YOU AND I, IT'S IN GOD'S PLAN

WHEN I'M WITH YOU, THERE ARE NO CANT'S, ONLY CAN'S

I REALLY LOVE YOU

OUR LOVE IS AS VAST AS THE SEA

I REALLY LOVE YOU

THE WOMAN OF MY DREAMS

SO JUST TAKE MY HAND

BY YOUR SIDE IS WHERE I'LL STAND

YOU AND ME, ME AND YOU

TOGETHER THERE'S NOTHING WE CAN'T DO

WHETHER WE'RE EXPLORING THE SEA OR TRAVELING TO THE MOON

I REALLY LOVE YOU

YES, ITS TRUE

I REALLY LOVE YOU

IF YOU TRUST ME

IF YOU TRUST ME WITH YOUR HEART

I'LL TRUST YOU WITH MY LIFE

I WANT TO WALK HAND IN HAND

FOREVER BY YOUR SIDE

IF YOU TRUST ME WITH YOUR HEART

I'LL TRUST YOU WITH MY MIND

I WILL HOLD YOU IN MY THOUGHTS

ALWAYS UNTIL I DIE

IF YOU TRUST ME WITH YOUR HEART

I'LL TRUST YOU WITH MINE TOO

WE CAN TRUST AND LOVE EACH OTHER

I'LL ALWAYS CHERISH YOU

LINGER

MY HEART, IT LONGS FOR YOU

WORDS JUST CAN'T EXPLAIN

AND I KNOW IT SEEMS STRANGE

BECAUSE OF YOUR PRESENCE, I AM NO LONGER THE
SAME

MY SOUL LONGS FOR YOU

WITHOUT YOU THERE'S ONLY PAIN

AND IT'S SO COLD

FEELS LIKE I'M STUCK IN THE RAIN

BUT MY MIND TELLS MY HEART TO REFUSE THE THOUGHT
OF YOU

IT TELLS ME TO OPEN MY EYES

WHAT WE HAD, IT DIED

WHAT DO I DO?

WHAT DO I CHOOSE?

CAN YOU BLAME ME?

HOW CAN I FORGET?

ALL THE GOOD TIMES THAT WE SPENT TOGETHER

THE THOUGHTS AND FEELINGS SEEM TO LINGER

LOVE ETERNAL

HOW LONG MUST I WAIT?

YOUR TOUCH AND YOUR EMBRACE

I DESIRE TO FEEL YOU

YOU CAUSE MY MIND TO GO INTO OVERDRIVE

EVERY TIME I THINK OF YOU BY MY SIDE

WITH YOU I WANT THAT REAL LOVE

AND FOR THAT I'M WILLING TO LAY DOWN MY PRIDE

THROUGH ALL OF THIS, HERE I AM

IMPATIENTLY WAITING

LONGING TO SEE YOUR FACE

TO KISS YOUR LIPS

WANTING TO MAKE UP FOR THE LOST TIME WE HAVEN'T EVEN SHARED

MY MIND SAYS I'M MISGUIDED

MY HEART DOESN'T EVEN CARE

SOUL MATES, LOVERS, MARRIED, LOVE ETERNAL

LOVE

ANY OF IT REAL?

WHAT I SEE

WHAT I FEEL

THE SENSATIONS

MY HEART FEELS WEIRD

SHOULD I TRUST IT?

THE OBVIOUS ELUDES ME

I'M STILL IN THE DARK

SITTING BACK WATCHING LIKE I'M AT THE MOVIES

REAL OR FICTION

I CAN'T TELL

WHAT IS THIS?

NOW I'M PANICKING

SOMETHING'S CHANGING

I DON'T UNDERSTAND IT

I REFUSE TO ADMIT WHAT COULD BE

WHAT'S THE PROBABILITY?

THIS IS A BIT STRANGE

MAKE ME OVER

LORD, MAKE ME OVER

MY LIFE, I WILL COMMIT TO THEE

MY HEART, MAKE IT STRONGER

TO BETTER SERVE YOU

LORD, MAKE ME OVER

I'M SO TIRED OF WHO I WAS

EVERY MISTAKE THAT I'VE MADE

IT PUSHED ME FURTHER AND FURTHER FROM YOU

LORD, MAKE ME OVER

I DESIRE A NEW LIFE IN YOU

CREATE ME IN YOUR IMAGE

WITHOUT SPOTS, WRINKLES, OR BLEMISHES

GIVE ME A NEW HEART

I WANT TO LOVE AGAIN

I'M TIRED OF TRYING TO PRETEND

I WANT YOU TO COME INTO MY LIFE

GIVE ME A NEW TONGUE

I WANT TO BOLDLY PROCLAIM THAT YOU ARE THE ONE

MY KING

LORD, MAKE ME OVER

MY PLEA

THE CRY OF MY HEART

HEAR IT, LORD

WIPE AWAY MY UNSEEN TEARS

COMFORT MY SOUL

THIS PAIN IS CRIPPLING

WITHOUT YOU I WOULD HAVE ALREADY BEEN CRUSHED

SORROWFUL

ALL THE WRONG I HAVE DONE

I CAN'T SEEM TO FORGIVE MYSELF

WHEN FACE TO FACE WITH MY DEFEAT, I COWER

AFRAID OF TRYING AGAIN BECAUSE OF THE POSSIBILITY OF FAILURE

WEAKNESS

MY OWN PROBLEMS KEEP ME CHAINED AND BOUND

GOD, DELIVER ME

THE CRY OF MY HEART

I WANT TO BE CLOSER TO YOU

I DON'T WANT LIFE TO GET IN THE WAY

THIS IS MY PLEA

Songs of Me

For you I have waited, suffered, and prayed

You, whose mind, soul, heart and body I desire

Whose laugh warms my heart

Skin as soft as the petals on the rarest flowers

Your scent intoxicates my very being, a natural aphrodisiac

In my eyes none can compare to you

You who fit into my arms

You hold my heart and turn it as you please

You are the most precious treasure I have

As we share breath and body

Chained by the one who ordained us

May we never part

The one I cherish

The very thought of you causes my heart to skip a beat

Blood rushes at the sound of your name

My virtuous woman

Nothing on earth can match your value

My weakness and my strength

May we always please and honor each other

Praying and uplifting each other before the lord

Beyond eternity

Thoughts

So much to say

So many thoughts swimming endlessly

Yet I am at a loss for words

Or rather I lack the words to describe the thoughts

How can you express a feeling that words can't describe?

My thoughts are wild and untamed

Coming and going as they please

Who knows where they come from

Chaotic it seems

Every thought doesn't have a place

Some are thrown out

Willingly discarded

Trust me, it's for the best

Of this I have no doubt

Maybe instead of describing them with words, colors would suffice

I know that's way too simple

But it would be oh so nice

I shall say what I can with these words that I have

Nothing more, nothing less

TORTURE

AGAIN, I SEE YOU IN MY DREAMS

ACTING JUST LIKE YOU DID WHEN WE USED TO BE

FOR A WHILE I THOUGHT IT WAS REAL

THEN I WAKE UP, CRASHING BACK INTO REALITY

ALL OF A SUDDEN, THE MEMORIES AND EMOTIONS COME
RUSHING BACK

AND NOW I'M DEPRESSED BECAUSE I KNOW,

I KNOW THAT I WOULD PREFER TO STAY IN A DREAM
WORLD THAN A REALITY WITHOUT YOU

IT SEEMS LIKE I AM BEING TAUNTED WITH MEMORIES OF
THE PAST WHEN I WISH I COULD FORGET

WHY ME?

WHEN WILL THIS TORTURE END?

ANGER

KEEP ME FAR AWAY FROM MY OWN WRATH

CLEAR MY MIND AND CALM MY SOUL

MAKE MY MIND THE STILL WATERS

GUARD ME FROM THOSE WHO WOULD DOUSE THE
FLAMES OF MY ANGER IN GASOLINE

EASE MY HEART

WHEN I WANT TO LASH OUT AND YELL

KEEP ME SILENT, EVEN IF THE ANGER IS JUSTIFIED

BRIDLE MY ANGER LIKE A HORSE

CHANGE MY THINKING OR MY CONDITIONS

BLOCK AND LOCK THE GATE THAT LEADS TO MY FURY

DAM UP MY ANGER SO THAT IT DOES NOT OVERFLOW,
DESTROYING MY PROGRESS

LET GENTLENESS AND PEACE CONSUME ME

DROWN AND SURROUND ME IN IT

I DON'T WANT TO SNAP

AFRAID

I AM AFRAID TO TRUST

I AM AFRAID OF THE THINGS YOU COULD SAY

I AM AFRAID OF US

EVERY TIME I OPEN UP AND TRUST, SOMETHING BAD
HAPPENS

I AM AFRAID OF GETTING HURT AGAIN

I AM AFRAID OF THE PAIN

I AM AFRAID THAT YOU WILL SEE ME AS JUST A FRIEND

I AM AFRAID THAT IT COULD ALL BE A GAME

CAN YOU PROVE TO ME

COMPLETELY

THAT I AM YOURS, AND THAT YOU LOVE ME?

I AM AFRAID

I AM AFRAID TO HOLD YOUR HAND

I AM AFRAID BECAUSE YOU COULD LET GO

I AM AFRAID TO LOVE

OR EVEN HOLD YOU CLOSE

I AM AFRAID THAT WE MIGHT BE A LIE

I AM AFRAID THAT I COULD BE YOUR JOKE

I'M AFRAID TO TELL YOU HOW I REALLY FEEL

I AM AFRAID TO HAVE HOPE

SO CAN YOU PROVE TO ME

COMPLETELY

THAT I AM YOURS, AND THAT YOU LOVE ME?

BECAUSE I AM AFRAID

Treasure

You are my treasure

I have spent so much time waiting and searching

Now that I've found you, it's like I'm in heaven

The glow and luster of your soul,

it has shown me life in a new light

I attempt to memorize your features so that I can
immortalize them in my memory

Your perfect smile, vibrant eyes, full cheeks, and luscious
lips

I've committed them all to memory

Shame on all those who have hurt and misused you in the
past

They did not know your value

But I do

Priceless

I wouldn't trade you for all the silver and gold in existence

My "I Do" will be forever, while we are young and when
we are old

You are more than just a trophy

You're my partner, my ride or die

I will always respect you

Protect you 'til I die

I'll invest in you as you invest in me

On this trip called life

It will get rough at times

But you are who I want and who I need

After searching for so very long,

I have finally found my treasure.

Voice

How do I find my voice in the crowd?

I'm just so quiet and they're all so very loud

I do my own thing

I seldom stick out

Yet my thoughts keep on racing

I'm so full of doubt

Always hesitating

Second guessing

Over thinking

Selling myself short, like I'm not even competing

Observing perspectives from others I believe are better

Inwardly panicking

I'm so introspective

You can tell me I'm good enough

But it's pointless if I don't believe it

Surrounded by talented people

With all their achievements

I don't want to compete

I just desire to be me

Confident and loud

Outgoing and free

Do I do more of this?

Should I say less of that?

Can I fake a big smile,

When deep down I'm sad?

What's my first step?

If I fail, then what's next

How do I manage these thoughts in my head?

How do I recover after harsh criticism?

What do I do when I want to shy away?

Or when there are tears in my eyes?

There's a pull in two directions

Step out and move forward

Definitely the riskier of the two choices

It's the uncertainty that scares me

I don't want to look like a fool

Then there's the second choice

The safe choice

The choice that represents complacency

Keep to myself

A potential talent that remains unnoticed

No risk, no reward, no growth

But no pain or worry either

A crossroad with differing futures that starts with a single question:

"How do I find my voice?"

Through A Child's Eyes

Pain, pain, pain

Why won't you just go away?

All I know is misery

I could really use a change

Mommy cries herself to sleep

Daddy had to go away

All I have left is his picture

Mommy says Uncle Sam took him away

I don't know what that means

But Uncle Sam sounds so mean

Traded Daddy for a folded flag

Now I only see him in my dreams

Mommy is gone more now

She works multiple jobs across town

We barely have any food to eat

I really miss my family

I hate going to school

It's so hard to focus

I have to force myself to try

Otherwise my imagination takes over

I imagine Mommy and Daddy

At home with me, happy and bonding

Then I come crashing back to reality

I'm all alone

Society Issues

We promote the violence

Then we wonder why

We have blood-soaked streets

And tear-filled eyes

Everyone is grieving

Communities are depleting

Jobs and daddies leaving

It's like our lives have no meaning

Justifying a culture of vultures

We are quick to yell out in rage

What happens when it's us that hurts us?

Epidemic illusion

Can't win because we loosen

Values and excuses

So far behind in the game

No wonder we keep losing

On edge around the police

Ain't safe in the hood

Unless homie say he know me

Double jeopardy

Families stay feuding

Playing who wants to be a millionaire

Got you covering up what they're doing

I already know

I'm guilty on sight

Be it Fox News or CNN

My skin determines my rights

Those who hold the power

Benefit of the system

Another child goes missing

Time passes and we forget them

We have Christians who are anti-Christ

Big pharma is anti-life

Pay you off to keep you silent

Promotion filled with lies

Pick your poison

Make a dollar

Stack it up

Bring ya boys in

Repeat the process

An empty promise

I'm going to make you rich

But first just buy this

The price keeps rising

Dreams just out of reach

So you believe the lies

Politicians protect corporations

Few care for the people

And if your help isn't being publicized

Then we won't see you

And why should anyone working a 9 to 5

Have to pinch pennies to stay alive?

Paid just enough

To keep your profits high

When the rich tell the poor how to live on less

So they can keep more

Cut costs

Screw the people

Greed-filled heart

Truly evil

Pass the cost onto others

Blame the market

Hide your money in offshore accounts

Claim you're a target

Bottom line is,

We all have to do better

Hold each other accountable

We're all in this together

There should never be a day

When a child is raped, sold, or goes hungry

When you have to decide between insurance or housing

When materials determine value

When power is abused to oppress those without a voice

This ain't ethics

This is humane

Blanket statements from closed minds never change

Every person that chooses to stay silent

Or turns the other way when they witness violence

Fear is one thing

But its apathy that's guiding

Until the shoe is on the other foot

Then you hate the silence

To those who are on the front line

Working hard but you don't make the headline

I salute you on behalf of those who are on the sideline

Endless hours

Little thanks

No compensation

You didn't change

Challenged injustice

You didn't sway

When things got hard

You didn't faint

You used your voice

Stood in the way

Thank you.

To Me

To me, your eyes are like the subtle glow of the moon on a clear night

To me, your smile is like the sun, able to brighten my darkest day

To me, your embrace is worth more than all the treasures this world has to offer

To me, not being with you feels like I'm missing part of my soul

To me, your value is as immeasurable as the stars in the night sky

To me, the depths of my love for you is far greater than the distance between the highest mountain and the deepest ocean

To me, you are worth the pain and heartache I have experienced

To me, you are more precious than diamonds, rubies, and gold

To me, you are someone who I would risk everything for

To me, no distance is too great to catch a glimpse of you

To me, the only future I can see is one where we are together

To me, we are destined by God and tethered with love

To me, your request is one that I can't refuse, because you have my heart There is almost nothing that I wouldn't do for you

To me, you are a physical manifestation of God's love for me

To me, you are strong

To me, you are kind

To me, you are as necessary for my life as the sun is for warmth

To me, you are the one.

I WISH

I wish I never met you

Never got to know you

Opened and revealed my soul to you

Back and forth, up and down

I was better off alone than with you around

I wish I could get back the time and energy wasted on you

I was the one helping you when I barely had enough for me

If you needed help, I was a text away

But a response from you would take days

I wish you could experience you from my point of view

I wish I could turn back time

You go your way and I'll go mine

I don't hate you,

But for the lesson you taught me, call me grateful

Because of you, I learned my own self worth

I wish I could talk to everyone who is experiencing what I did with you

I wish I could tell them to walk away

Delete their number and block their page

I wish I knew then what I know now

I'm worth more than you could give

Message to the Church People

Our youth has been deceived

Trust me, it's a fact

Few are trying to hear about Jesus

They would rather have cash and a good time

See, they don't want to hear how he suffered, bled, and died

Too busy tryna live fast, get cash, have sex, and get high

And I know that nobody wants to say it, but we all know that it's true

This world is twisted and sick, heading toward certain doom

The saying "Cash Rules Everything Around Me," or Cream

But I would rather have a Goat

God Over All Things

And I know that I am different, I expect the opposition

But I was called to be like Christ, so it's time for a name change

Let me introduce myself as Christian

See, I choose to take a stand

If this world is like a lion

Then as Christians we should be like lambs

And Since God is our protector

We are safest in his hands

But I get it, no one wants to hear that

Our world is full of modern-day warlocks and witches

Played over radio waves commanding us to bow down

Snitching, we refuse, it's a well-known unspoken rule

Until the situations are reversed

We try our best to find the answers

Don't forget, not snitching is the rule

And many of these so-called church folks ain't much better

Using the Bible to spread hate and condemn

Whatever happened to love and the same grace and
mercy that saved them?

"You ain't dressed right," "You're a sinner," "You don't
belong."

But correct me if I'm wrong

Wasn't it Jesus who said "Let he who is without sin cast
the first stone"?

But no one wants to hear that

Let's focus on the spiritual and then work on the physical

Stop attempting to be like man when Christ is the pinnacle

With experience comes wisdom and it should follow age

So, when the older ones tell us something

Let's hear what they have to say

Yet not every old person is wise

Us young people know this to be true

We don't want things sugar coated

Yet force-feeding just won't do

But I get it, no one wants to hear that

In conclusion, the world is a mess

The poor are oppressed

The sick keep getting sicker

While the rich could care less

But God is our solid rock and on him we will stand

He is our healer and provider

Our lives are in his hands

Biography

Douglas Uriah Sloss was Born on Tuesday, June 4, 1991, to Doug and Tammy Sloss in the city of Muncie, Indiana. He enjoyed writing and even received praise from his teachers for his outlandish subject matters for free writing assignments.

He grew up in a loving home with his parents as well as his younger brother and sister. His faith has always played a big role in his life and continues to do so. Currently, he's a Technical Sergeant in the United States Air Force and a firefighter in the city of East Chicago. He enjoys spending time with his pets, family, and friends when he is able.

He began writing poetry, stories, and songs in his early twenties and continues to do so, with more than 300 original pieces. He values familial relationships and loyalty. Even though he is currently single, he has seen the way his father and mother love and value each other even when things are difficult.

His first book, titled "This Is Me," is a collection of select poems that he has written and compiled.

Made in the USA
Monee, IL
09 July 2021